Defoe Abbott Marx Hardy Melville Machiavelli Montaigne Chesterton Cooper Emerson Joyce Austen Hugo Eliot Grimm
Stoker Carroll Christie Molière
Wilde Maupassant Haggard Byron Schiller
Garnett Einstein Fitzgerald Engels Smith Kafka Hall
Goethe Hawthorne Dostoyevsky Willis
Cotton Kipling Doyle
Baum Henry Nietzsche Balzac
Leslie Dumas Flaubert Turgenev Vatsyayana Crane
Stockton Verne
Burroughs Whitman Gogol Vinci
Curtis Tocqueville Busch
Homer Widger Tolstoy
Darwin Thoreau Twain Scott Plato
Potter Freud Zola Lawrence Dickens Harte
Kant Jowett Stevenson Hesse
Andersen Burton
London Descartes Cervantes Voltaire
Poe Aristotle Wells
Hale James Hastings Cooke
Bunner Shakespeare Irving
Richter Chambers da Shaw Wodehouse Alcott
Doré Dante Chekhov Benedict
Swift Pushkin Newton

 tredition®

tredition was established in 2006 by Sandra Latusseck and Soenke Schulz. Based in Hamburg, Germany, tredition offers publishing solutions to authors and publishing houses, combined with world-wide distribution of printed and digital book content. tredition is uniquely positioned to enable authors and publishing houses to create books on their own terms and without conventional manufacturing risks.

For more information please visit: www.tredition.com

TREDITION CLASSICS

This book is part of the TREDITION CLASSICS series. The creators of this series are united by passion for literature and driven by the intention of making all public domain books available in printed format again - worldwide. Most TREDITION CLASSICS titles have been out of print and off the bookstore shelves for decades. At tredition we believe that a great book never goes out of style and that its value is eternal. Several mostly non-profit literature projects provide content to tredition. To support their good work, tredition donates a portion of the proceeds from each sold copy. As a reader of a TREDITION CLASSICS book, you support our mission to save many of the amazing works of world literature from oblivion. See all available books at www.tredition.com.

Project Gutenberg

The content for this book has been graciously provided by Project Gutenberg. Project Gutenberg is a non-profit organization founded by Michael Hart in 1971 at the University of Illinois. The mission of Project Gutenberg is simple: To encourage the creation and distribution of eBooks. Project Gutenberg is the first and largest collection of public domain eBooks.

Beside Still Waters

Arthur Christopher Benson

Imprint

This book is part of TREDITION CLASSICS

Author: Arthur Christopher Benson
Cover design: Buchgut, Berlin – Germany

Publisher: tredition GmbH, Hamburg - Germany
ISBN: 978-3-8472-1286-7

www.tredition.com
www.tredition.de

BESIDE
STILL WATERS

BY

ARTHUR CHRISTOPHER BENSON

FELLOW OF MAGDALENE COLLEGE, CAM-BRIDGE

"I will run the way of Thy commandments;
when Thou hast set my heart at liberty."

FOURTH IMPRESSION

LONDON
SMITH, ELDER, & CO., 15 WATERLOO PLACE
1910

Printed by BALLANTYNE, HANSON & Co.
At the Ballantyne Press, Edinburgh

CONTENTS

BESIDE STILL WATERS

I

The Family — The Scene — The Church —
Childhood — Books

Hugh Neville was fond of tender and minute retrospect, and often indulged himself, in lonely hours, with the meditative pleasures of memory. To look back into the old years was to him like gazing into a misty place, with sudden and bright glimpses, and then the cloud closed in again; but it was not only with his own life that he concerned himself; he liked to trace in fancy his father's eager boyhood, brought up as he had been in a great manufacturing town, by a mother of straitened means, who yet maintained, among all her restrictions, a careful tradition of gentle blood and honourable descent. The children of that household had been nurtured with no luxuries and few enjoyments. Every pound of the small income had had its appointed use; but being, as they were, ardent, emotional natures, they had contrived to extract the best kind of pleasure out of books, art, and music; and the only trace that survived in Hugh's father of the old narrow days, was a deep-seated hatred of wastefulness and luxury, which, in a man of generous nature, produced certain anomalies, hard for his children, living in comparative wealth and ease, to interpret. His father, the boy observed, was liberal to a fault in large matters, but scrupulously and needlessly particular about small expenses. He would take the children on a foreign tour, and then practise an elaborate species of discomfort, in an earnest endeavour to save some minute disbursements. He would give his son a magnificent book, and chide him because he cut instead of untying the string of the parcel. Long after, the boy, disentangling his father's early life in diaries and letters, would wish, with a wistful regret, that he had only had the clue to this earlier; he would have sympathised, he thought, with the idea that lay beneath the little economies, instead of fretting over them, and discussing them rebelliously with his sisters. His father was a man of almost passionate affections; there was nothing in the world that he more desired than the company and the sympathy of his children; but he had, besides this, an intense and tremulous sense of responsibility towards them. He attached an undue importance to small indications of character; and thus the children were seldom at ease with their father, because he rebuked them constantly, and found frequent fault, doing almost violence to his tenderness, not from any pleasure in censoriousness, but from a terror, that was almost morbid, of the consequences of the unchecked development of minute tendencies.

Hugh's mother was of a very different disposition; she was fully as affectionate as his father, but of a brighter, livelier, more facile nature; she came of a wealthy family, and had never known the hard discipline from which his father had suffered. She was a good many years younger than her husband; they were united by the intensest affection; but while she devoted herself to him with a perfect understanding of, and sympathy with, his somewhat jealous and puritanical nature, she did not escape the severity of his sense of responsibility, and his natural instinct for attempting to draw those nearest to him into the circle of his high, if rigid, standards. Long afterwards, Hugh grew to discern a greater largeness and liberality in her methods of dealing with life and other natures than his father had displayed; and no shadow of any kind had ever clouded his love and admiration for his mother; his love indeed could not have deepened; but he came gradually to discern the sweet and patient wisdom which, after many sorrows, nobly felt and ardently endured, filled and guided her large and loving heart.

His father, after a highly distinguished academical career, entered the Church; and at the time of Hugh's birth he held an important country living together with one of the Archdeaconries of the diocese.

Hugh was the eldest child. Two other children, both sisters, were born into the household. Hugh in later days loved to trace in family papers the full and vivid life which had surrounded his unconscious self. His mother had been married young, and was scarcely more than a girl when he was born; his father was already a man grave beyond his years, full of affairs and constantly occupied. But his melancholy moods, and they were many, had drawn him to value with a pathetic intentness the quiet family life. Hugh could trace in old diaries the days his father and mother had spent, the walks they had taken, the books they had read together. There seemed for him to brood over those days, in imagination, a sort of singular brightness. He always thought of the old life as going on somewhere, behind the pine-woods, if he could only find it. He could never feel of it as wholly past, but rather as possessing the living force of some romantic book, into the atmosphere of which it was possible to plunge at will.

And then his own life; how vivid and delicate the perceptions were! Looking back, it always seemed to be summer in those days. He could remember the grassy walks of the pleasant garden, which wound among the shrubberies; the old-fashioned flowers, sweet-williams and Canterbury-bells, that filled the deep borders; the rose-garden, with the pointed white buds, or the big-bellied pink roses, full of scent, that would fall at a touch and leave nothing but an orange-seeded stump. But there had been no thought of pathos to him in those years, as there came to be afterwards, in the fading of sweet things; it was all curious, delightful, strange. The impressions of sense were tyrannously strong, so that there was hardly room for reflection or imagination; there was the huge chestnut covered with white spires, that sent out so heavy a fragrance in the spring that it was at last cut down; but the felling of the tree was a mere delightful excitement, not a thing to be grieved over. The country was very wild all round, with tracts of heath and sand. The melodious buzzing of nightjars in hot mid-summer evenings, as they swept softly along the heather, lived constantly in his memory. In the moorland, half a mile away, stood some brick-kilns, strange plastered cones, with blackened tops, from which oozed a pungent smoke; those were too terrible to be visited alone; but as he walked past with his nurse, it was delightful and yet appalling to look into the door of the kiln, and see its fiery, glowing heart. Two things in particular the boy grew to love; one was the sight of water in all its forms; a streamlet near the house trickled out of a bog, full of cotton-grass; there were curious plants to be found here, a low pink marsh-bugle, and the sundew, with its strange, viscid red hands extended; the stream passed by clear dark pools to a lake among the pines, and fell at the further end down a steep cascade; the dark gliding water, the mysterious things that grew beneath, the fish that paused for an instant and were gone, had all a deep fascination for the boy, speaking, as they seemed to do, of a world near and yet how far removed from his own!

And then still more wonderingly, with a kind of interfusion of terror and mystery, did he love the woodlands of that forest country. To steal along the edge of the covert, with the trees knee-deep in fern, to hear the flies hum angrily within, to find the glade in spring carpeted with blue-bells—all these sights and sounds took hold of his childish heart with a deep passion that never left him.

All this life was, in memory, as I have said, a series of vignettes and pictures; the little dramas of the nursery, the fire that glowed in the grate, the savour of the fresh-cut bread at meal-times, the games on wet afternoons, with a tent made out of shawls and chairs, or a fort built of bricks; these were the pictures that visited Hugh in after days, small concrete things and sensations; he could trace, he often thought, in later years, that his early life had been one more of perception than of anything else; sights and sounds and scents had filled his mind, to the exclusion of almost all beside. He could remember little of his relations with those about him; the figures of the family and servants were accepted as all part of the environment. The only very real figure was the old nurse, whose rare displeasure he had sorrowed over more than anything else in the world, and whose chance words, uttered to another servant and overheard by the child, that she was thinking of leaving them, had given him a deeper throb of emotion than anything he had before known, or was for many years to know.

But the time for the eager and romantic association with other people, which was to play so large a part in Hugh's life, was not yet come. People had to be taken as they came, and their value depended entirely upon their kindness or unkindness. There was no sense of gratitude as yet, or desire to win affection. If they were kind, they were unthinkingly and instinctively liked. If they thwarted or interfered with the child's little theory of existence, his chosen amusements, his hours of leisure, his loved pursuits, they were simply obstacles round which his tiny stream of life must find its way as it best could.

There was indeed one other chief delight for the child: the ordered services of the Church hard by the house. He loved with all his heart the fallen day, the pillared vault, the high dusty cornices, the venerable scent; and the services, with their music solemn and sweet, the postures of the ministers, the faces, clothes, and habits of the congregation—all was a delightful field of pleasing experience. Yet religion was a wholly unreal thing to the child. He learnt his Bible lessons and psalms; he knew the liturgy by heart; but the religious idea, the thought of God, the Christian life of effort, were all things that he merely accepted as so many facts that were taught him, but without the least interest in them, or even the shadowiest attempt to apply them to his own life. It seemed strange to Hugh when, in years long after, religion came to have so deep a meaning to him, that it should have been so entirely a blank to him in the early days. God was no more to him than a far-off monarch; a mighty and shadowy person, very remote and powerful, but the circle of whose influence never touched his own. And yet one of the deepest desires of his father's mind had been to bring a sense of religion home to his children. Hugh used to wonder how he had missed it; but the practical application of religion, to which the Bible lessons had led up, had been to the child a mere relief from the tension of thought, because at last he had escaped from the material teaching about which he might be questioned, and which he would be expected to remember.

Personal relations, then, had scarcely existed for Hugh as a child. Older and bigger people, armed with a vague authority, had to be obeyed, and the boy had no theory which could account for their inconsequent behaviour; they were amiable or ill-humoured, just or unjust; he never attempted to criticise or condemn them by a moral standard; he simply accepted them as they were, and kept as much as possible out of the way of those who manifested sharpness or indifference. With children of his own age it was in many ways the same, though there seemed to the boy to be more hope of influencing their behaviour; threats, anger, promises, compliance could be applied; but of the affection that simply desired to please the object of its love, the boy knew nothing. Once or twice he went away from home on a visit, and because he wept on his departure, he was supposed to have a tender and emotional nature; but it was not tenderness, at least not tenderness for others, that made him weep. It was partly the terror of the unknown and the unfamiliar; it was partly the interruption to the even tenor of his life and the customary engagements of his day; and in this respect the boy had what may be called a middle-aged temperament, an intense dislike of any interference with his own ways; he had no enterprise, none of the high-hearted enjoyment of novelty, unless he was surrounded by a bulwark of familiar personalities; but partly, too, his love was all given to inanimate things; and as he drove out of the gate on one of these visits, the thought that the larches of the copse should be putting out their rosy buds, the rhododendrons thrusting out their gummy, spiky cases, the stream passing slowly through its deep pools, the bee-hive in the little birch avenue beginning to wake to life, and that he should not be there to go his accustomed rounds, and explore all the minute events of his dear domain—it was this that brought out the tears afresh, with a bitter, uncomforted sense of loss and bereavement.

So the early years passed for the boy, in a dream full to the brim of small wonders and fragrant mysteries. How pleasant it was to sink to sleep on summer evenings with the imagination of voyaging all night in a little boat or carriage; how delightful to wake, with the morning sun streaming in at the window, to hear the casement ivy tap on the pane, and to rehearse in the mind all the tiny pleasures of the long day! His short lessons were easy enough for the boy; he was quick and acute, and had a good memory; but he took not the smallest interest in them, except the interest of making a situation go smoothly; the only interest was in the thought of the unmolested lonely play that was to follow. He cared little for games, though they had a certain bitter excitement, the desire of emulation, the joy of triumph about them. He loved best an aimless wending from haunt to haunt, an accumulation of small treasures in places unknown to others; and most of all the rich sense of observation of a hundred curious and delicate things; the nests of birds in the shrubbery, the glossy cones of the young pines, the green, uncurling fingers of the bracken, the fresh green sword-grass that grew beneath the firs; he did not care to know the nature or the reasons of these things; it was enough simply to see them, to explore them with restless fingers, to recognise their scents, hues, and savours, with the sharp and unblunted perceptions of childhood.

Then came the intellectual awakening. Hugh's mother, who had an extraordinary gift for improvisation, began to tell the children stories in the nursery evenings; and these tales of giants and fairies grew to have an extreme fascination for the child; not that he peopled his own world with them, as some imaginative children do; the boy's perceptions were too definite for that; such beings belonged to a different region; he had no idea that they existed, or had ever existed. They belonged to the story world, which was associated in his mind with bright fires and toys put away, when he nestled as close as he could to his mother's knee, with her hand in both his own, exploring every ring and every finger, till he could recall, many years after, each turn and curve, and even each finger-nail of those dear hands. And then at last came the supremest joy of all; the children used to be summoned down to their mother's room, and she began to read aloud *Ivanhoe* to them; and then indeed a new world, a world that had really existed, sprang to light.

Hugh used to wonder afterwards how much he had really understood of what was read; but the whole thing seemed absolutely alive to him; his pictorial fancy came into play, and the details of woods and heaths that he knew so well began to serve him in good stead; and then the child, who had before thought of reading as merely a tiresome art that he was forced to practise, found that it was the key that admitted him into this wonderful world. It did not indeed destroy his relish for the outer world of nature, for at all hours of the day, when it was possible to slip out of doors, he went his solitary way, looking, looking; until every tree and flower-border and thicket of the small domain became so sharply imprinted upon the mind that, years after, he could walk in memory through the sunny garden, and recall the minutest details with an astonishing accuracy.

But books became for the child a large part of his life. It was a story that he desired, something that should create a scene for him, personalities like or unlike his own, whose deeds and words he could survey, leaning, so it seemed to him, from a magic casement into the new scene. His father, whose taste was for the improving in literature, was willing enough that the boy should be supplied with books, but hardly understood that the child was living in a world of bright fancies and simple dreams. His father, moreover, who had all his life had a harder and more definite turn of thought, and had desired knowledge of a precise kind, wanted the boy to read the little dry books, uncouthly and elaborately phrased, that had pleased himself in his own early days. Hugh's mind was precise enough; but these terse biographies, these books of travel, these semi-scientific stories seemed to Hugh only to relate the things that he did not want to know. His father had been born at a time when the interest in the education of children was first taking shape, the days of Miss Edgeworth's *Frank*, and *Harry and Lucy*, that strange atmosphere of gravity and piety, when children were looked upon as a serious responsibility more than as a poetical accessory to life; not as mysterious and fairy-like creatures, to be delicately wooed and tenderly guided, but rather as little men and women, to be re- pressed and trained, and made as soon as possible to have a sense of responsibility too. Hugh used to look at the old books in later days, and wonder what the exact social position of the parents in such books as *Frank*, and *Harry and Lucy*, were supposed to be. They lived in the country; they were not apparently wealthy; they lived with much simplicity. Yet Harry's father seemed to have nothing to do but to conduct his children over manufactories, and to take them long walks—in the course of which he diligently improved their minds by a species of Socratic inquiry. But Hugh never thought of quarrelling with the books provided; he seized upon any trace of humanity or amusement that they afforded, any symptoms of char- acter and liveliness, and simply evaded the improving portion, which blew like a dry wind over his spirit. When his father talked over the books with the child, he listened tolerantly to the boy's amusement at how the cake had rolled down the hill, or how the little pig had got into the garden; but he was disappointed that the boy seemed not to care whether the stone which Harry threw de- scribed a parabola or not, though there was an odious diagram to explain it, full of dotted lines and curves. Yet the boy held on his way, deaf to all that did not move him or interest him, and fixing jealously on all that fed his fancy. Such books as *Grimm's Fairy Tales* and *Masterman Ready* were wells of delight, enacted as they were in a strange and exciting world; and he was sensitive, too, to the beauty of metre and sonorous phrases, learning poetry so easily that it was supposed to be a species of wilfulness in him that the Collects and texts, and the very Psalms — that seemed to him so unreal and husk-like then, and that later became to him like fruits full of refreshment and savour and sweet juices — found their way so slowly into his memory, and were so easily forgotten.

II

The Schoolmaster — School Life — Companions

The time came for Hugh to go to school. He drifted, it seemed to him afterwards, with a singular indifference and apathy of mind, into the new life, though the parting from home was one of dumb misery; not that he cared deeply, as a softer-hearted child might have cared, at being parted from his father, his mother, his sisters. People, even those nearest to the boy, were still only a part of the background of life, a little nearer perhaps, but hardly dearer, hardly more important than trees and flowers, except that a greater part of his life was spent with them. But the last afternoon in the familiar scene — it was a hot, bright September day — tried the boy's fortitude to the uttermost. He felt as though the trees and walks would almost miss his greeting and presence — and what was the saddest part of all to him was that he could not be sure of this. Was the world that he loved indifferent to him? Did it perhaps not heed him, not even perceive him? He had always fancied that these trees and flowers had a species of sight, that they watched him, the trees shyly out of their green foliage, the flowers with their bright unshrinking gaze. The tallest trees seemed to look down on him from a height, regarding him with a dignified and quiet interest; his personal affection for them had led him indeed to be careful not to ill-use them; he had always disliked the gathering of flowers, the tearing off of boughs or leaves from shrubs. They seemed to suffer injury patiently, but none the less did he think that they were hurt. He liked to touch the full-blown heads of the roses, when they yielded their petals at a touch into his hand, because it seemed that they gave themselves willingly. And then too, when the big china bowl that stood in the hall was full of them, and they were mixed with spices, the embalming process seemed to give them a longer and a fuller life.

But now he was leaving all this; day after day the garden would bloom, until the autumn came, and the trees showered down their golden leaves on walk and lawn. He had seen it year after year, and now he would see it no more. Would they miss him as he would miss them? And so the last afternoon was to him a wistful valediction; he went softly about, to and fro, with a strange sadness at his heart, the first shadow of the leave-takings of the world.

The school to which he went was a big place in the suburbs of London, standing near a royal park. The place was full of dignified houses, standing among trees and paddocks, with high blank garden-walls everywhere. The school itself had been once a great suburban mansion, the villa of a statesman. The rooms were large, high, and dignified, but the bareness of life, under the new conditions, was a great trial to the boy. He had a certain luxuriousness of temperament, not in matters of meat and drink, but in the surroundings and apparatus of life. The bare, uncurtained, uncarpeted rooms, the big dormitory with its cubicles, the stone-flagged passages, all appeared to him mean and sordid. His schoolmaster was a man of real force of character, a tall stately personage, with a great enthusiasm for literature, a fine converser and teacher, and with a deep insight into character. But this was marred by a want of tenderness, a certain harshness of disposition, and a belief that boys needed to be repressed and dragooned. Hugh conceived an overwhelming terror for this majestic man, with the dress and bearing of a fine gentleman, with his flashing eyes, his thin lips, his grey curly hair, his straggling beard. He was a friend of Hugh's father, and took a certain interest in the boy, especially when he discovered that, though dreamy and forgetful, Hugh's abilities were still of a high order. His work was, in fact, always easy to him, though he was entirely destitute of ambition. Certain scenes impressed themselves on the boy's mind with extraordinary vividness. Mr. Russell, the schoolmaster, used to read out every week a passage for the boys to turn into verse. He read finely, and Hugh noticed, with a curious surprise, that Mr. Russell was almost invariably affected to tears by his reading. But, on the other hand, a scene which he saw, when he and certain other boys were waiting to have their exercises looked over, was for years a kind of nightmare to him. There was a slow and stupid boy in the class, whom Mr. Russell chose to consider obstinate, and who was severely caned, in the presence of the others, for mistakes in his exercise. Even ten years after, Hugh could remember with a species of horror the jingling of the keys in Mr. Russell's pocket, as he took them out to unlock the drawer where the cane lay. Perhaps this proved a salutary lesson for Hugh, for the terror that such an incident might befall himself, caused him to take an amount of trouble over his exercises which he would certainly not otherwise have bestowed.

On Sunday evenings Mr. Russell read aloud to the upper boys in his drawing-room; and this was a happy time for Hugh; he loved to sit in a deep chair, and feast his eyes upon the pictures, the china, the warm carpet and curtains of the fire-lit room, and the books that he heard read had a curious magic for him. Mr. Russell never seemed to take any particular notice of him, and Hugh used to feel that he was despised for his want of *savoir faire*, his slovenliness, his timidity; and it was a great surprise to discover, long after, a bundle of letters from Mr. Russell to his father, in which he found his abilities and shortcomings discussed with extraordinary penetration.

Hugh played no games at his school; there was not then the organisation of school games which has since grown up. His favourite occupation was wandering about the big grounds, to which certain boys were admitted, or joining in the walks, which a dozen boys, conducted by a peevish or good-tempered usher, as the case might be, used to take in the neighbourhood of the school. The high garden-walls, with the mysterious posterns, the huge horse-chestnuts looking over the leaded tops of the classical arbours with which the grounds of an adjacent villa were adorned; the great gate-posts of the main entrances, the school-house itself, looking grimly down from a great height, all these held strange mysteries for the boy, sinking unconsciously into his spirit.

But he made very few friends either with masters or boys. He had none of the merry sociability of childhood; he confided in no one, he simply lived his life reluctantly, hating the place, never sure that some ugly and painful punishment, some ridicule or persecution might not fall on him out of a clear sky for some offence unconsciously committed. He had hardly a single pleasant memory connected with the school, except of certain afternoons when the boys who had done well for the week were allowed to go without supervision to the neighbouring shops, and purchase simple provender. But if he made no friends, he at least made no enemies; he was always friendly and good-tempered, and he was preserved by his solitariness from all grossness and evil. It was a big school, and occasionally he perceived in the talk and behaviour of his companions the signs of some ugly and obscene mystery that he did not understand, and that he had no wish to penetrate. But the result, which in after days surprised him with a sense of deep gratitude and thankfulness, was, that though he spent two years at this school, he left it with absolutely untainted innocence, such innocence as in later days he would have held to be almost inconceivable, as to all the darker temptations of the senses. But the absence of close human relationship was the strange thing. He had a few boys with whom he associated in a familiar way. But he had no idea of the homes from which they came, he knew nothing of their inner taste and fancies. And though his own feelings and interests were definite enough and even strong, though he read books of all kinds with intense avidity, he never spoke of them to other boys, while at the same time he was averse to writing letters home; his father complained once in the holidays that he knew nothing of what the boy did at school. Hugh could not put into words what he felt to be the truth, namely, that he hardly knew himself. He submitted quietly and obediently to the dull routine of the place, and felt so little interest in it, that he could not conceive that his father should do so either. There were of course occasional exciting incidents, but to relate them would have required so much explanation, such a list of personages, such a description of circumstances, that he felt unable to embark upon it. His father asked him whether he would not like some of his school friends to visit him at home, and he rejected the suggestion with a kind of incredulous horror. The thought of invading the sanctity, the familiarity of home, with the presence of a boy who might reveal its secrets to others, was too appalling to face; it hardly occurred to him that the boys had homes of their own, places which they loved. He only thought of them as figures on the school stage, to be conciliated, tolerated, lived with, his only preoccupation being to shield and guard his own heart and inner life from any intruding influence whatever. He had no desire ever to see one of the crew again, boys or masters. Some indeed were preferable to others, but no one could be trusted for an instant; the only safe course was to make no claim, and to shield oneself as far as possible against all external influences, all alliances, all relationships.

Hugh, in after life, could hardly recall the faces of any of his companions; the only way at the time in which he differentiated them to himself was that some looked kinder than others — that was the only thing that mattered. Thus the years dragged themselves along, the school-time hated with an intensity of dislike, the holidays eagerly welcomed as a return to old pursuits. The boy used to lie awake in the big dormitory in the early summer mornings, thinking with vague terror and disquiet of the ordered day of labour that lay before him. There were peacocks kept in the grounds, whose shrill feminine screams of despairing reproach were always inseparably connected with the dreariness of the place. His last morning at the school he woke early, full of joyful excitement, and heard the familiar cries with a thankful sense that he would never hear them again. He said no good-byes, made no farewell visits. He waved his hand, as he drove away, in merry derision at the grim high windows that looked down on the road, the only thought in his mind being the feeling of unconquerable relief that the place would see him no more.

He used to wonder, in after days, whether this could have been avoided; whether it was a wholesome discipline for a child of his age and his perhaps peculiar temperament to have been brought up under these conditions. After all, it is the case of the average boy that has to be considered, and for the average boy, insouciant, healthy-minded, boisterous, there is probably little doubt that the barrack-life of school has its value. Probably too for Hugh himself, though it did not in any way develop his intellect or his temperament, it had a real value. It taught him a certain self-reliance; it showed him that what was disagreeable was not necessarily intolerable. What Hugh needed to make him effective was a certain touch of the world, a certain hardness, which his home life did not tend to develop. And thus this bleak and uncheered episode of life gave him a superficial ordinariness, and taught him the need of conventional compliance with the ways of the mysterious, uninteresting world.

III

The Public School — Friendships — The Opening Heart — The Mould — The Last Morning

The change was accomplished, and Hugh went to a public school. In later life, conscious as he became of the strain and significance of personal relations with others, he used to wonder at the careless indifference with which he had entered the big place which was to be his home for several years, and was to leave so deep a mark upon him. In his mature life, in the case of the official positions he was afterwards to hold, unimportant though they were, the thought of his relations to those with whom he was to work, the necessity of adapting himself to their temperaments, of establishing terms of intercourse with them, used to weigh on his mind for many days before the work began. But here, he reflected, where life was lived on so much closer terms, when the words and deeds, the feelings and fancies of the boys, among whom he was to live, were of the deepest and most vital importance, he entered upon the new life, dull and careless, without interest or excitement, simply going because he was sent, just dumbly desirous of ease and tranquillity. He had been elected on to the foundation of an ancient school, and the surroundings of the new place did indeed vaguely affect him with a sort of solemn pleasure. The quaint mediaeval chambers; the cloisters, with their dark and mysterious doorways; the hall, with its high timbered roof and stained glass; the huge Tudor chapel, with its pure white soaring lines; the great organ, the rich stall-work, and the beautiful fields with their great elms—all this gave him a dim delight. He was taken to school by his father, who was full of affection, hope, and anxiety. But it seemed to Hugh, with the curiously observant power that he already possessed, though he could not have put it into words, that his father, rather than himself, was experiencing the emotion that it would have been appropriate for him to have felt. His father was disappointed that Hugh did not seem more conscious of membership, of the dignity and greatness of the place. His tender care about the books, the pictures, and the furnishing of Hugh's little room, did indeed move the boy to a certain gratitude. But his father's way on such occasions was to order what he himself would have liked, and his taste was severe; and then he demanded that the boy should not only accept, but enthusiastically like, what was given him. Hugh's immature taste was all for what was bright and fanciful; his father's for what was grave and dignified; and thus though the boy was glad to have pictures of his own, he had rather that they had not been engravings of old religious pictures; and he would have preferred dainty china objects, such as candlesticks and ornaments, to the solid metal fittings which his father gave him. When they parted, his father gave him a serious exhortation to which the child hardly listened. He set him on his guard against certain temptations, when Hugh was ignorant of what he was alluding to; and the emotion with which the boy took leave of his father was rather of envy that he was returning to the dear home life, than regret at being parted from him.

The first two years of the boy's school life passed like a bewildered dream; he had a companion or two, but hardly a friend; he had little idea of what was going on in the big place round him; he was not in the least ambitious of distinction either in work or games; his one desire was not to be conspicuous in any way. He was now a shy, awkward creature; but as he was good-humoured enough, and as his performances excited no envy in any of his companions, he was left to a great extent to his own devices. The masters with whom he was brought into contact he regarded with a distant awe; it never occurred to him that they took any interest in their work or in the characters of the boys they dealt with. He supposed vaguely that they liked to show their power by scoring under the mistakes in exercises, and by setting punishments. But they were all dim and inhuman beings to him. Only very gradually did it dawn upon the boy that he had a place in a big society. He was habitually unsuccessful in examinations, but he became a proficient in football, which gave him a certain small consequence. He began to give thought to his clothes, and to adopt the customary tone of talk, not because he felt in sympathy with it, but because it was a convenient shield under which he could pursue his own ideas. But his tastes were feeble enough; he spent hours in the great school library, a cool panelled room, and though he had no taste for anything that was hard or vigorous, he read an immense amount of poetry and fiction. He began, too, to write poetry, with extraordinary precautions that his occupation should not be discovered. He was present on one occasion when a store of poems, the work of a curious and eccentric boy of his own age, was discovered in the drawer of a bureau. These were solemnly read aloud by a small tormentor, while the unhappy author, writhing with shame and misery, was firmly held in a chair, and each composition received with derisive comments and loud laughter. Hugh had joined, he remembered with a sense of self-reproach, in the laughter and the criticisms, though he felt in his heart both interest in and admiration for the poems. But he dare not so far brave ridicule as to express his feelings, and simply fell, tamely and ungenerously, into the general tone. He did indeed make feeble overtures afterwards to the author, which were suspiciously and fiercely repelled, and the only practical lesson that Hugh learnt from the scene was to conceal his own literary experiments with a painful caution.

But as the years passed there came a new influence into Hugh's life. He had always been observant, in his quiet way, of other boys, and at last, as his nature developed, he began to idealise them in a romantic way. The first object of his admiration was a boy much older than himself, an independent, graceful creature, who had a strong taste for beautiful things, and adorned his room with china and pictures; he was moreover a contributor of verses to the school magazine, which seemed to Hugh models of elegance and grace.

But he was far too shy to think of attracting the notice of his hero. It simply became an intense preoccupation to watch him, in chapel or hall; it was a fearful joy to meet him, and he used to invent excuses for passing his room, till he knew the very ornaments and pictures by sight. That room seemed to him a kind of sacred shrine, where a bright being lived a life of high and lofty intellectual emotion. But he never succeeded in exchanging a word with the object of his admiration, except on a certain day, marked in his calendar long after with letters of gold. There was a regatta in the neighbourhood of the school, to which the boys were allowed to go under certain conditions. He had gone, and had spent his day in wandering about alone, until the glare and the crowd had brought on a headache; and he had resolved to return home by an early train. He went to the station, hoping that he might be unobserved, and stepped into an empty carriage. Just as the train started, he heard rapid steps; the door was flung open, and his hero entered. Seeing a junior boy of his own house in the carriage, he made some good-natured remark, and before Hugh could realise the greatness of his good fortune, his hero had sate down beside him, and after a few words, with a friendly impulse, had launched into a ghost story which lasted the whole of the journey, and the very phrases of which haunted Hugh's mind for weeks. They had walked down from the station together, but alas for the vicissitudes of human affairs, his god, contented with having shown courteous kindness to a lonely and uninteresting small boy, never gave him for the rest of the school term, after which he left, the slightest sign of recognition; and yet for years after the fields and trees and houses which they had passed on the line were suffused for Hugh with a subtle emotion in the memory of that journey.

And then, a little later than this, Hugh had the first and perhaps the most abiding joy of his life. A clever, ambitious, active boy of his own standing, whom he had long secretly admired, took a pronounced fancy to him. He was a boy, Hugh saw afterwards, with a deeply jealous disposition; and the first attraction of Hugh's friendship had been the fact that Hugh threatened his supremacy in no department whatever. Hugh was the only boy of the set who had never done better than he in anything. But then there came in a more generous feeling. Hugh's heart awoke; there was nothing which it was not a pleasure to do for his friend. He would put anything aside, at any moment, to walk, to talk, to discharge little businesses, to fetch and carry, to be in attendance. Moreover, Hugh found his tongue, but his anxiety to retain his friend's affection made him astonishingly tactful and discreet. He was always ready to sympathise, to enter into any suggestion; he suppressed himself and his own tastes completely and utterly; and he found too, to his vast delight, that he could be entertaining and amusing. The books he had read, the fiction with which he had crammed himself, his keen eye for idiosyncrasies and absurdities, all came to his assistance, and he was amply repaid by a smile for his trouble.

The two boys became inseparable, and perhaps the thing that made those days of companionship bright with a singular and golden brightness, was that there was in his friend the same fastidious vein, the same dislike of any coarseness of talk or thought which was strong in Hugh. Looking back on his school life, with all the surprising foulness of the talk of even high-principled boys, it was a deep satisfaction to Hugh to reflect that there had never been in the course of this friendship a single hint, so far as he could recollect, in their own intercourse with each other, of the existence of evil. They had tacitly ignored it, and yet there had not been the least priggishness about the relationship. They had never inquired about each other's aspirations or virtues, in the style of sentimental schoolbooks. They had never said a word of religion, nor had there ever been the smallest expression of sentiment. All that was taken for granted. It was indeed one of those perfect, honest, wholesome companionships, which can only exist between two cheerful boys of the same age. Hugh indeed was conscious of a depth of sacred emotion, too sacred to be spoken of to any one, even to be expressed to himself. It was not, in fact, a definite relation which he represented to himself; it was rather like a new light shed abroad over his life; incidents had a savour, a sharp outline which they had lacked before. He became conscious, too, of the movement and intermingling of personal forces, of characters. He no longer had the purely spectatorial observation of others which had distinguished him before, but beheld other personalities, as in a mirror, in the mind of his friend. And then, too, what was a far deeper joy, literature and poetry began to yield up their secrets to him. Poetry had been to him before, a gracious, soulless thing like a tree or a flower, and had been apprehended purely in its external aspect. But now he suddenly saw the emotion that burnt beneath, not indeed of the love that is mingled with desire—that had still no meaning for the soul of the boy, or only the significance of a far-off mystery; but he perceived for the first time that it was indeed possible to hold something dearer than oneself, one's country, one's school, one's friend—something large and strong, that could intervene between one's hopes and oneself.

Hugh was indeed not yet, if ever, to learn the force of these large words—patriotism, honour, self-surrender, public spirit; he remained an individualist to the end. His country never became for him the glowing reality that it means for some. It was dear because his friends, who were also Englishmen, were dear; and his school for the same reason. If he had a friend in the School Eleven Hugh would always rather that his friend should be distinguished than that the school should win. He could not disentangle the personal fibre, or conceive of an institution, a society, apart from the beings of which it was composed.

But his friendship broke in pieces, once and for all, the dumb isolation in which he had hitherto lived. It opened for him the door of a larger and finer life, and his soul, endowed with a new elasticity, seemed to leap, to run, to climb, with a freshness and vigour that he had never before so much as guessed at.

The closeness of this friendship gradually loosened—or rather the exclusive companionship of its earlier stages grew less; but it seemed to Hugh to bring him into new relations with half the world. He became a boy with many friends. Other boys found his quaint humour, his shrewd perceptions, his courtesy and gentleness attractive. He took his new-found popularity with a quiet prudence, a good-humoured discretion that disarmed the most critical; but it was deeply delightful to the boy; he seemed to himself to have passed out of the shadow into the sun and air. Life appeared to be full of gracious secrets, delightful emotions, excellent surprises; it became a series of small joyful discoveries. His intellect responded to the stimulus, and he became aware that he had, in certain directions, a definite ability of which he had never suspected himself.

The only part of his nature that was as yet dark and sealed was the religious spirit. In a world so full of interests and beauties, there was no room for God; and at this period of his life, Hugh, with a blindness which afterwards amazed him, grew to think of God in the same way that he unconsciously thought of his father, as a checking and disapproving influence, not to be provoked, but equally not to be trusted. Hugh had no confidences with his father; he never felt sure, if he gave way to easy and unconstrained talk with him, that his father would not suddenly discern something of levity and frivolity in his pursuits; and this developed in Hugh a gentle hypocrisy, that was indeed the shadow of his sympathy, which made him divine what would please his father to talk about. He found all his old letters after his father's death, arranged and docketed—the thought of the unexpected tenderness which had prompted this care filled his eyes with sudden tears—but how un-real they seemed! There was nothing of himself in them, though they were written with a calculated easiness of expression which made him feel ashamed.

And it was even the same with his idea of God. He never thought of Him as the giver of beautiful things, as the inspirer of happy friendships; he rather regarded Him as the liberal dispenser of dis-appointments, of rainy days, of reproofs, of failures. It was natural enough in a place like a public school, where the masters set the boys an example of awkward reticence on serious matters. Even Hugh's house-master, a conscientious, devoted man, who, in the time of expansion, was taken into the circle of his sincere friend-ships—even he never said a serious word to the boy, except with a constrained and official air as though he heartily disliked the sub-ject.

It is no part of this slender history to trace the outer life of Hugh Neville. It must suffice to say that, by the time that he rose to the top of the school, he appeared a wholesome, manly, dignified boy, quiet and unobtrusive; very few suspected him of taking anything but a simple and conventional view of the scheme of things; and indeed Hugh's view at this time was, if not exactly conventional, at least unreflective. It was his second time of harvest. He had gathered in, in his childhood, a whole treasure of beautiful and delicate impres-sions of nature. Now he cared little for nature, except as a quiet background for the drama which was proceeding, and which absorbed all his thoughts. What he was now garnering was impressions of personalities and characters, the odd perversities that often surprisingly revealed themselves, the strange generosities and noblenesses that sometimes made themselves felt. But an English public school is hardly a place where these larger and finer qualities reveal themselves, though they are indeed often there. The whole atmosphere is one of decorum, authority, subordination. Introspection is disregarded and even suppressed. To be active, good-humoured, sensible, is the supreme development. Hugh indeed got nothing but good out of his school-days; the simple code of the place gave him balance and width of view, and the conventionality which is the danger of these institutions never soaked into his mind; convention was indeed for him like a suit of bright polished armour, in which he moved about like a youthful knight. He left school curiously immature in many ways. He had *savoir faire* enough and mild literary interests, but of hard intellectual robustness he had nothing. The studies of the place were indeed not of a nature to encourage it. The most successful boys were graceful triflers with ancient literatures; to write a polished and vapid poem of Latin verse was Hugh's highest accomplishment, and he possessed the power of reading, with moderate facility, both Latin and Greek; add to this a slender knowledge of ancient history, a slight savour of mathematics, and a few vague conceptions of science; such was the dainty intellectual equipment with which he prepared to do battle with the great world. But for all that he knew something of the art of dealing with men. He had learnt to obey and to command, to be deferential to authority and to exact due obedience, and he had too a priceless treasure of friendship, of generous emotion, untinged with sentimentality, that threw a golden light back upon the tall elms, the ancient towers, the swiftly-running stream. It was to come back to him in later years, in reveries both bitter and sweet, how inexpressibly dear the place had been to him; indeed when he left his school, it had simply transmuted itself into his home,—the Rectory, with its trees and walks, its narrower circle of interests, having faded quite into the background.

The last morning at school was filled with a desolation that was almost an anguish; he had packed, had distributed presents, had said a number of farewells, each thrilled with a passionate hope that he would not be quite forgotten, but that he might still claim a little part in the place, in the hearts so dear to him. He lay awake half the night, and in the dawn he rose and put his curtain aside, and looked out on the old buttresses of the chapel, the mellow towers of the college, all in a clear light of infinite brightness and freshness. He could not restrain his tears, and went back to his bed shaken with sobs, yet aware that it was a luxurious sorrow; it was not sorrow for misspent days; there were carelessnesses and failures innumerable, but no dark shadows of regret; it was rather the thought that the good time was over, that he had not realised, as it sped away, how infinitely sweet it had been, and the thought that it was indeed over and done with, the page closed, the flower faded, the song silent, pierced the very core of his heart. One more last thrill of intense emotion was his; his carriage, as he drove away, surmounted the bridge over the stream; the old fields with the silent towers behind them lay beneath him, the home of a hundred memories. There was hardly a yard of it all that he could not connect with some little incident; the troubles, the unhappinesses, such as they had been, were gone like a shadow; only the joy remained; and the memory of those lost joys seemed like a bird beating its wings in the clear air, as it flew to the shadow of the pines. What was to follow? he cared little to think; all his mind was bent on the sweet past. Something of the mystery of life came home to him in that moment. He would have readily died then, he felt, if a wish could have brought him death. Yet there was nothing morbid in the thought; it was only that death seemed for a moment a fitting consummation for the end of a period that had held a richness and joy that nothing else could ever hold again.

IV

Undergraduate Days — Strain — Recovery — A First Book

The desire to be returning to school with which Hugh went up to the university did not last long; he paid a visit to his housemaster, and saw with a mixture of envy and amusement how his juniors had all stepped quietly into the places which he and his friends had vacated, and were enjoying the sensation of influence and activity. He was courteously treated and even welcomed; but he felt all the time like the *revenante* of Christina Rossetti,—"I was of yesterday." And then too, a few weeks after he had settled at Cambridge, in spite of the strangeness of it all, in spite of the humiliation of being turned in a moment from a person of dignity and importance into a mere "freshman," he realised that the freedom of the life, as compared with the barrack-life of school, was irresistibly attractive. He had to keep two or three engagements in the day, and even about these there was great elasticity. The independence, the liberty, the kindliness of it all, came home to him with immense charm. And then, too, the city full of mediaeval palaces, the quiet dignity, the incomparable beauty of everything, gave him a deep though partly unconscious satisfaction. But for the first year he was merely a big schoolboy in mind. The real change in his mental history dated from his election to a small society which met weekly, where a paper was read, and a free discussion followed. Up to this time Hugh's religion had been of a purely orthodox and sensuous description. He had grown up in an ecclesiastical atmosphere, and the ritual of Church Services, the music, the ceremonial, had been all attractive to him. As for the dogmatic side, he had believed it unquestioningly, just as he had believed in the history or the science that had been taught him. But in this society he met young men—and older men too, for several of the Dons were members—who were rationalists, materialists, and definitely sceptical. It dawned on his mind for the first time that, while all other sciences were of a deductive kind, endeavouring to approach principles from the observation and classification of phenomena, from the scrutiny of evidence, that theology was a science based on intuitions, and dependent on assumptions which it was impossible to test scientifically. The first effect of this was to develop a great loyalty to his traditions, and almost the first hard thinking he had ever done was in the direction of attempting to defend his faith on scientific principles. But the attempt proved fruitless; one by one his cherished convictions were washed away, though he never owned it, not even to himself. He was regarded as a model of orthodoxy. He made friends with a young Fellow of his college, who was an advanced free-thinker, and set himself to enlighten the undergraduate, whose instinctive sympathy gave him a charm for older men, of which he was entirely unconscious. They had many serious talks on the subject; and his friend employed a kind of gentle irony in undermining as far as he could the foundations of what seemed to him so irrational a state of mind. One particular conversation Hugh remembered as vividly as he remembered anything. He and his friend had been sitting, one hot June day, in the college garden, then arrayed in all its midsummer pomp. They sate near a great syringa bush, the perfume of which shrub in later years always brought back the scene before him; overhead, among the boughs of a lime-tree, a thrush fluted now cheerfully, now pathetically, like one who was testing a gift of lyrical improvisation. The elder man, wearied by a hard term's work, displayed a certain irritability of argument. Hugh held tenaciously to his points; and at last, after a silence, his friend turned to him and said, "Well, after all, it reduces itself to this; have you an interior witness to the truth of what you say, which you can honestly hold to be superior to the exterior evidences of its improbability?" Hugh smiled uneasily, and conscious that he was saying something which he hoped rather than knew, said, "I think I have." The older man shrugged his shoulders and said, "Then I can say no more!"— nor did he ever again revert to the question, from what Hugh thought was a real generosity and tenderness of spirit.

All the time Hugh practised a species of emotional religion, attending the chapel services devoutly, even willingly hearing sermons. There was a little dark church, in a tiny courtyard hemmed in by houses, and approached by a narrow passage, served by a Fellow of a neighbouring college, who preached gentle devotional discourses on Sunday evenings, to which many undergraduates used to go. These were a great help to Hugh, because they transferred religion from the intellectual to the spiritual region; and thus, though he was gradually made aware of the weakness of his intellectual position, he continued his religious life, in the hope that the door of a mystery might some day be opened to him, and that he might arrive, by an inner process, at a conviction which his intellect could not give him. But here as elsewhere he was swayed by a species of timidity and caution. While on the one hand his intellect told him that there was no sure and incontrovertible standing-ground for the orthodoxy which he professed, yet, on the other hand, he could not bear to relinquish the chance that certainty might be found on different lines.

In the middle of these speculations, he suffered a dark experience. He fell, for the first time in his life, into ill-health. His vitality and nervous force were great, and though soon depleted were soon recuperated; but the new and ardent interests of the university had appealed to him on many sides; he worked hard, took violent exercise, and filled up every space of time with conversation and social enjoyment; he had no warning of the strain, except an unaccustomed weariness, of which he made light, drawing upon his nervous energy to sustain him; the wearier he grew, the more keenly he flung himself into whatever interested him, learning, as he thought, that the way to conquer lassitude was by increased exertions, the feeling of fatigue always passing off when he once grew absorbed in a subject. He took to sitting up late and rising early, and he had never seemed to himself more alert and vigorous in mind, when the collapse came. He was suddenly attacked, without warning, by insomnia.

One night he went to bed late, and found it difficult to sleep; thoughts raced through his brain, scenes and images forming and reforming with inconceivable rapidity; at last he fell asleep, to awake an hour or two later in an intolerable agony of mind. His heart beat thick and fast, and a shapeless horror seemed to envelop him. He struck a light and tried to read, but a ghastly and poisonous fear of he knew not what, seemed to clutch at his mind. At last he fell into a broken sleep; but when he rose in the morning, he knew that some mysterious evil had befallen him. If he had been older and wiser, he would have gone at once to some sensible physician, and a short period of rest would probably have restored him; but the suffering appeared to be of so purely mental a character, that he did not realise how much of it was physical. For that day and for many days he wrestled with a fierce blackness of depression, which gradually concentrated itself upon his religious life; he became possessed by a strong delusion that it was a punishment sent to him by God for tampering with freedom of thought, and little by little a deep moral anxiety took hold of him. He searched the recesses of his heart, and ended by painting his whole life in the blackest of colours.

In the endeavour to find some degree of peace, he read the Scriptures constantly, and the marks he made in his Bible against verses which seemed to hold out hope to him or to plunge him into despair, remained through the after years as signs of this strange conflict of mind. His distress was infinitely increased by attending some services at a Mission which then happened to be proceeding which, instead of inspiring him with hope, convinced him that his case was past recovery. For some weeks he tasted, day by day, the dreary bitterness of the cup of dark and causeless depression, and laboured under an agonising dejection of spirit. This intensity of suffering seemed to shake his whole life to its foundation. It made havoc of his work, of his friendships, of the easy philosophy of his life. He began to learn the distressing necessity of dissembling his feelings; he endeavoured at great cost to bear as unconcerned a part as before in simple festivities and gatherings, while the clouds gathered and the thunder muttered in his soul. And all the time the answer never came. Wrestle as he might, there seemed to him an impenetrable barrier between him and the golden light of God. He learnt in what dark and cold isolation it is possible for the soul to wander. Slowly, very slowly, the outlook brightened; a whole range of new emotions opened before him. The expressions of suffering and sorrow, that had seemed to him before but touching and beautiful phrases, became clear and vivid. His own powers of expression became more subtle and rich. And thus, though he gradually drifted back into a species of spiritual epicureanism, he always felt grateful for his sojourn in the dark world. He did not abandon his religious profession, but he became more content to suspend his judgment. He saw dimly that the mistake he had made was in hoping for anything of the nature of certainty. He became indeed aware that the only persons who are indubitably in error, are those who make up their minds in early life to a theory about God and the world, and who from that moment admit no evidence into their minds except the evidence that supports their view. Hugh saw that life must be, for him at all events, a pilgrimage, in which, so long as his open-mindedness, his candour, his enthusiasm did not desert him, there were endless lessons to be learnt by the way. And thus he came back gratefully and wearily to his old life, his old friendships. His college became to him a very blessed place; apart from the ordinary social life, from the work and the games which formed a background and framework in which relationships were set, he found a new region of desires, impulses, ideas, through which he wandered at his will.

At this time Hugh could not be said to be happy. The shadows of his dark moods often hung about him, and he bore in his face the traces of his suffering. He felt, too, that he had failed in his religious quest, though side by side with this was the consciousness that he had been meant to fail. His religious views were a vague Theism, coupled with a certain tendency to determinism, to which his wanderings had conducted him. Christian determinism he called it, because though his old unquestioning view of the historical evidences of Christianity had practically disappeared, yet his belief in Christian morality as the highest system that had yet appeared in the world was unshaken. And it was at this time, just after taking his degree, that he wrote a little book, a species of imaginary biography which attained, to his surprise, a certain vogue. The book was an extraordinarily formless and irrelevant production, written upon no plan, into which he shovelled all his vague speculations upon life. But its charm was its ingenuous youthfulness and emotional sincerity; and although he afterwards came to dislike the thought of the book so much, that at a later date he bought up and destroyed all the copies of it that remained unsold, yet for all that it had the value of being a perfectly sincere revelation of personality, and represented a real, if a sentimental, experience. The book was severely reviewed, but as it was published anonymously, this gave Hugh little anxiety; and so he shouldered his burden, and went out of the sheltered life into the wilderness of the world.

V

Practical Life — The Official World — Drudgery — Resignation — Retirement

There will be no attempt made here to trace in any detail the monotonous years of Hugh's professional life, because they seemed to him to have been in one sense lost years; there was at all events no conscious growth in his soul. His spirit seemed to him afterwards to have lain, during those years, like a worm in a cocoon, living a blind life. Externally, indeed, they were the busiest time of his life. He became a hard-worked official in the Civil Service. He lived in rooms in London. He spent his day at the office, he composed innumerable documents, he wrote endless letters; he seemed to himself, in a way, to be useful; he did not dislike the work, and he found it interesting to have to get up some detailed case, and to present it as lucidly as possible. He began his official life with an intention of doing some sort of literary work as well; but he found himself incapable of any sustained effort. Still, he continued to write; he did a good deal of reviewing, and kept a voluminous diary, in which he scribbled anything that struck him, recording scenes, conversations, impressions of books and people. This he found was easy enough, but it seemed impossible to complete anything, or to give it a finished form. However, he acquired the habit of writing, and gained some facility of expression. His short holidays were spent either in travel, with some like-minded companion, or in his quiet country home, where he read a large number of books, and lived much in the open air. But his progress seemed to have been purely intellectual. He lost his interest in abstract problems and in religious matters, which retired to a remote distance, and appeared to him to be little more than a line of blue hills on a distant horizon, as seen by a man who goes up and down in a city. He had visited them once, those hills of hope, and he used to think vaguely of visiting them again; but meanwhile the impulse and the opportunity alike failed him.

Yet in another sense he did not consider those days lost. He gained, he used to feel afterwards, a knowledge of the world, a knowledge of men, a knowledge of affairs. This contact with realities took from his somewhat dreamy and reflective temperament its unpractical quality. If he chose afterwards to leave what is commonly called the world, it was a deliberate choice, founded on a thorough knowledge of its conditions, and not upon a timid and awkward ignorance. He did not leave the world because it frightened or bewildered him, but because he did not find in it the things of which he was in search. Neither, on the other hand, did he quit the life of affairs like a weakling or an inefficient person who had failed in it, and had persuaded himself that incompetence was unworldliness. Hugh became a remarkably efficient official, alert, sensible, practical, and prudent. He was marked out for promotion. He was looked upon as a man who got on well with inferiors and superiors alike, who could be trusted to do a complicated piece of business well, who was worth consulting.

Moreover he acquired a very serviceable and lucid style, a power of clear statement, which afterwards stood him in good stead. His official work gave him the power of seeing the point, it gave him an economy of words, an effective briskness and solidity of presentment; at the same time his literary work prevented him from degenerating into a mere précis-writer.

It is very difficult to say which of the days of a man's life are wasted and which are fruitful. It is not necessarily the days in which a man gives himself up to his chosen work in which he makes most progress. Sometimes a long inarticulate period, when there seems to a man to be a dearth of ideas, a mental drought, acts as a sort of incubation in which a thought is slowly conceived and perfected. Sometimes a long period of repression stores force at high pressure. The lean years are often the prelude, even the cause, of the years of fatness, when the exhausted and overteemed earth has lain fallow and still, storing its vital juices.

Sometimes, too, a disagreeable duty, undertaken in heaviness and faithfully fulfilled, rewards one by an increase of mental strength and agility. A painful experience which seems to drown a man's whole nature in depression and sadness, to cloud hope and eagerness alike, can be seen in retrospect to have been a period fertile in patience and courage.

Hugh did not find his official life depressing, but very much the reverse. He enjoyed dealing with affairs and with men. He used sometimes to wonder, half regretfully, half comfortably, at the fading of his old dreams, in which so much that was beautiful was mingled with so much that was uneasy. He began indeed to be somewhat impatient of sentiment and emotion, and to think with a sort of compassion of those who allowed themselves to be ruled by such motives. He did not exactly adopt a conventional standard, but he found it easier to live on a conventional plane, until he even began to be viewed by some of his old friends as a man who had adopted a conventional view. Hugh indeed found, in his official life, that the majority of those among whom his lot was cast, did seem whole-heartedly content to live in a conventional world and to enjoy conventional successes. Such men, and they were numerous, never seemed disposed to probe beneath the surface of things, unless they were confronted by adverse circumstances, bereavements, or indifferent health; and, under these conditions, their one aim seemed to be to escape as soon as possible from the region of discomfort: they viewed reflection as a sort of symptom of failing vitality. And so Hugh drifted to a certain extent into feeling that self-questioning and abstract thought were a species of intellectual ill-health. One arrived at no solution, any more than one did in the case of a toothache; the one thing to do was to get rid of the unsatisfactory conditions as swiftly as possible.

During this period of his life Hugh made many acquaintances, but no great friends. In fact the idea of close and intimate relationship with others fell more and more into the background; he became interested rather in the superficial and spectatorial aspect of things and persons. He began to see how differences of character and temperament played into each other, and formed a resultant which merged itself in the slow current of affairs. But he seemed to himself to be acquiring and sorting tangible experiences, and to have little speculative interest at all; he neither craved to make or to receive confidences. The hours not occupied by business were given to social life and to reading; and he was, or fancied himself to be, perfectly contented.

But as the years went on, instead of sinking into purely conventional ways, Hugh found a mood of dissatisfaction growing upon him. He found that after his holidays he came back with increasing reluctance to his work. The work itself, how unsatisfactory it became! Half the time and energy of the office seemed to be spent on creating rather than performing work; an immense amount of detail seemed to be entirely useless, and to cumber rather than to assist the conduct of the business that was important. Of course much of it was necessary work which had to be done by some one; but Hugh began to wonder whether his life was well bestowed in carrying out a system of which so much seemed to consist in dealing with unimportant minutiae, and in amassing immense records of things that deserved only to be forgotten. He found himself reflecting that life was short, and that he tended to spend the greater part of his waking hours in matters that were essentially trivial. He began to question whether there was any duty for him in the matter at all, and by what law, human or divine, a man was bound to spend his days in work in the usefulness of which he did not wholly believe.

Living, as he did, an inexpensive life of great simplicity, he had contrived to save a certain amount of money, and he was surprised to find how fast it accumulated. When he had been some fifteen years in his office, a great-uncle of his died, leaving Hugh quite unexpectedly a sum of a few thousand pounds, which, together with his savings, gave him a small but secure competence, as large, in fact, as the income he was accustomed to spend.

Even so, he did not at once decide to leave his official career. It seemed to him at first that the abandonment of a chosen profession ought not to depend upon the fact that one could live independently without it; he felt that there ought to be a better reason for pursuing a certain course of life than mere livelihood. But his accession of means enabled Hugh to give up all literary hack-work, such as reviewing, which had long been somewhat of a burden to him; he had found himself of late agreeing more and more with William Morris's doctrine, that there was something degrading in a man's printing his opinions about other persons' books for money; and he now began to indulge in more ambitious literary schemes. This involved him in a good deal of reading; but he found himself thwarted at every turn by the pressure of official business. He found that his reading had to be done over and over again; that he would master a section of his subject, and then for lack of time be compelled to put it aside, until it had passed out of his mind and needed to be recovered.

At last he made up his mind that he would take the first obvious opportunity that offered itself, to end his official work. It came in the form of an offer which, a year or two before, would have gratified his ambition, and which would have bound him without question to official work for the rest of his active life; he was offered in very complimentary terms the headship of a newly created department. He not only declined it, to the surprise and disappointment of his chief, but he resigned his appointment at the same time. He had a somewhat painful interview with the head of the office, who told him that he was sacrificing a brilliant and honourable career at the very moment when it was opening before him. Hugh did not, however, hesitate; he found it a difficult task to explain to his superior exactly what he intended to do, who expressed a good-humoured contempt for the idea of making a mild literary experiment, at an age when literary success seemed unattainable. The great man, indeed, one of whose virtues was an easy frankness, said that it seemed to him as absurd as if Hugh had expressed the intention of devoting the rest of his life to practising the piano or drawing in water-colours. Hugh was quite aware that his literary position was of a dilettante kind, and that he had done nothing to justify the hope that success in literature was within his reach. He pleaded that the service of the State was encumbered by a mass of unnecessary detail, in the usefulness of which he did not believe. The Secretary said that of course there was a good deal of drudgery, but that the same applied to most lives of practical usefulness; and he pointed out that by accepting the new appointment, Hugh would be set free to attend to work of a more original and important kind. But Hugh felt himself sustained by a curiously inflexible determination, for which he could not wholly account; he merely said that he had considered the question in all its bearings, and that his mind was made up; upon which the Secretary shrugged his shoulders, and said that he did not wish to over-persuade him; and that indeed, if Hugh accepted the new post merely in deference to persuasion, it would be good neither for himself nor for the service. He added a few conventional words to the effect that the office would be sorry to lose so courteous and competent an official; and Hugh recognised that his chief, with the instinct of a thoroughly practical man, had dismissed him from his thoughts, as an entirely fantastic and wrong-headed person.

His retirement was not unattended by pain; he found that the announcement of his departure aroused more surprise and sorrow among his colleagues than he had expected; it was depressing, too, to say good-bye to the well-known faces, the familiar rooms, the routine that formed so substantial a part of his life. But he found in himself a wholly unanticipated courage, and even a secret glee at the prospect of his release, which revealed to him how congenial it was. He cleared up the accumulations of years; he made his adieux with much real emotion; yet it was a solemn rather than a sad moment when he put his papers away for the last time, and handed over the keys of the familiar boxes to his successor. He went slowly down the stairs alone, and stopped at the door to say good-bye to the old attendant, whom he never remembered to have seen absent from his place. The old man said, "Well, sir, I did think as you would not have left us yet." Hugh replied, smiling, "Well, we have all to move on when our time comes, and I hope I leave only friends behind me." The old man seemed much affected by this, and said, "Yes, sir, we shall be glad to see you whenever you can look in upon us"—and then with much fumbling drew out and presented a small pen-wiper to Hugh, which he had made with his own hands—"and God bless you, sir!" he added, with an apology for the liberty he was taking. This was the only incident in his leave-taking which affected Hugh to tears; but they were tears of emotion, not of regret. He was looking on to the new life, and not back to the old; and as he went out into the foggy air, and along the familiar pavement, there was nothing in his heart that called him back. He was grateful for all the kindness and affection of his friends, and the thought that he held a place in their hearts. What he hoped, he hardly knew; but the release from the burden of the tedious and useless work was like that which Christian experienced, when the burden rolled from his back into the grave that stood in the bottom, and he saw it no more.

VI

His Father's Friendship—His Sister's Death— The Silent River

One of the best things that Hugh's professional life had brought him was a friendship with his father; their relations had been increasingly tense all through the undergraduate days; if Hugh had not been of a superficially timorous temperament, disliking intensely the atmosphere of displeasure, disapproval, or misunderstanding, among those with whom he lived, there would probably have been sharp collisions. His father did not realise that the boy was growing up; active and vigorous himself, he felt no diminution of energy, no sense of age, and he forgot that the relations of the home circle were insensibly altering. He took an intense interest in his son's university career, but interfered with his natural liberty, expecting him to spend all his vacations at home, and discouraging visits to houses of which he did not approve. He was very desirous that Hugh should ultimately take orders, and was nervously anxious that he should come under no sceptical influences. The result was that Hugh simply excluded his father from his confidence, telling him nothing except the things of which he knew he would approve, and never asking his advice about matters on which he felt at all keenly; because he knew that his father would tend to attempt to demolish, with a certain bitterness and contempt, the speculations in which he indulged, and would be shocked and indignant at the mere beckoning of ideas which Hugh found to be widely entertained even by men whom he respected greatly. His father's faith indeed, subtle and even beautiful as it was, was built upon axioms which it seemed to him a kind of puerile perversity to deny. Religion came to him in definite and traditional channels, and to seek it in other directions appeared to him a species of wanton profanity.

The result was an entire divergence of thought, of which Hugh was fully conscious; but it did not seem to him that there was anything to be gained by candid avowal. He was at one with his father in the essential doctrines of Christianity; and being by nature of a speculative turn, he considered the discrimination of religious truth, the criticism of religious tradition, to be rather a stimulating and agreeable mental pastime than a question of ethics or morals. Thus he was led into practising a kind of hypocrisy with his father in matters of religion. He felt that it was not worth while engaging in argument of a kind that would have distressed his father and irritated himself, upon matters which he believed to be intellectual, while his father believed them to be ethical. Hugh often pondered over this condition of things, which he felt to be unsatisfactory, but no solution occurred to him; he said to himself that he valued domestic peace rather than a frank understanding upon matters to which he and his father attached a wholly different value. But meantime he drifted further and further away from the ecclesiastical attitude, though his fondness for ecclesiastical art and ceremony effectually disguised from his father the speculative movement of his mind.

But his independent entrance upon his professional life had given him an emancipation of which he was not at first fully conscious. He did not act from set purpose, and only became aware later that if he had thought out a diplomatic scheme of action, he could not have devised a more effectual one. He simply made his own arrangements for the holidays; he travelled, he paid visits; he came home when it was convenient to him; but the result was that in the early years of his professional life he was very little at home. Hugh supposed afterwards that his father must have felt this deeply; but he did not show it, except that suddenly, almost in a day and an hour, Hugh became aware that their relations had completely altered. He found himself met with a deference, a courteous equality which he had never before experienced. Instead of giving him advice, his father began to ask it, and consulted him freely on matters which he had hitherto kept entirely in his own hands. The result was at once an extraordinary expansion of affection and admiration on Hugh's part. He realised, as he had never done before, the richness and energy of his father's mind within certain limits, his practical ability, his high-mindedness, his amazing moral purity. Once freed from the subservient relation imposed upon him by habit, Hugh saw in his father a man of real genius and effectiveness. The effectiveness he had hitherto taken as a matter of course; he had thought of his father as effective in the same way that he had thought of him as severe, dignified, handsome—it had seemed a part of himself; but he now began to compare his father with other men, and to realise that he was not only an exceptional man, but a man with a rare intensity of nature, whose whole life was lived on a plane and in an atmosphere that was impossible to easy, tolerant, conventional natures. He realised his father's capacity for leadership, his extraordinary and unconscious influence over all with whom he came in contact, the burning glow of his fervid temperament, his scorn and detestation of all that was vile or mean. It did not at once become easier for Hugh to speak freely of what was passing in his own mind; indeed he realised that his father was one of those whose prejudices were so strong, and whose personal magnetism was so great, that not even his oldest and most intimate friends could afford to express opposition to him in matters on which he felt deeply. But Hugh saw that he must accept it as an unalterable condition of his father's nature, and realising this, he felt that he could concede him an honour and a homage, due to one of commanding moral greatness, which he had never willingly conceded to his paternal authority. The result was a great and growing happiness. Sometimes indeed Hugh made mistakes, beguiled by the increasing freedom of their intercourse; he allowed himself to discuss lightly matters on which he could hardly believe that any one could feel passionately. But a real and deep friendship sprang up between the two, and Hugh was at times simply astonished at the confidence which his father reposed in him. There were still, indeed, days when the tension was felt. But Hugh became aware that his father made strong efforts to banish his own depression and melancholy when he was with his son, that it might not cloud their intercourse. Signs such as these came home to Hugh with intense pathos, and evoked an affection which became one of the real forces of his life. His father had consented to Hugh's entering the Civil Service, but he continued to hope that his son might ultimately decide to take orders; he had cherished that hope from Hugh's earliest years, and seeing Hugh's fondness for the externals of religion, while he knew nothing of his mental attitude, he still believed and prayed that Hugh might be led to enter the service of the Church. Hugh realised that this was still his father's deep preoccupation, and perceived that he avoided any direct expression of his wishes, exercising only a transparent diplomacy which was infinitely touching—so touching indeed that Hugh sometimes debated within himself whether he might not so far sacrifice his own bent, which was more and more directed to the maintenance of an independent attitude, in order to give his father so deep and lasting a delight. But he was forced to decide that the motive was not cogent enough, and that to adopt a definite position, involving the suppression of some of his strongest convictions, for the sake of giving one he loved a pleasure, was like exposing the ark to the risks of battle. He knew well enough that if he had declared his full mind on the subject to his father, the extent to which he felt forced to suspend his judgment in religious matters, his father would have desired the step no longer.

With the rest of the family circle, in these years, Hugh's relations were affectionate but colourless. With his natural reticence, he shrank from speaking of the thoughts which predominated in his mind; especially while there was an abundance of interesting and uncontroversial topics which afforded endless subjects of conversation; and the tendency to leave matters alone which, if debated, might have caused distress, was heightened by the death of one of Hugh's sisters.

She was a girl of a very deep, loyal, and generous nature, full of activities and benevolences, and at the same time of a reflective order of mind. She had been a strong central force in the family; and Hugh found it strange to realise, after her death, that each member of the family had felt themselves in a peculiar relation to her, as the object of her special preoccupation. The event, which was strangely sudden, stirred Hugh to the bottom of his soul. The vacant chair, the closed loom, the sudden cessation of a hundred activities, brought sharply to his mind the dark mystery of death. That a door should thus have been suddenly opened, and one of the familiar band bidden to enter, and that the loving heart that had left them should be unable to communicate the slightest hint of its presence to those who desired her in vain, seemed to him a horrible and desperate thing. For the first time in his life the terrible secrets of identity opened before his eyes. He could not bring himself to believe in the extinction of so vital, so individual a force, but he recognised with a mournful terror that, so far as scientific evidence went, the whole preponderating force of facts tended to prove that the individuality was, if not extinguished, at least merged in some central tide of life, and that the only rebutting evidence was the cry of the burdened heart that dared not believe a possibility so stern, so appalling. He wrestled dumbly and darkly against these sad convictions, and how many times, in miserable solitude, did he send out a wistful prayer that, if it were possible, some hint, some slender vision might be granted him as a proof that one so dear, so desired, so momently missed, was still near him in spirit. But no answer came back from the dark threshold, and, leaning in, he could but discern a landscape of shapeless horror, in which no live thing moved by the shore of a grey and weltering sea. Little by little a dim hint came to comfort him; he thought of all the unnumbered generations of men who had lived their brief lives in sun and shade, full of hopes and schemes and affections. One by one they had lain down in the dust. In the face of so immutable, so absolute a law, it seemed that rebellion and questioning was fruitless. God gives, God takes away, He makes and mars, He creates, He dissolves; and if we cannot trust the Will that bids us be and not be, what else in this shifting world, full of dark secrets, can we trust? It cannot be said that this thought comforted Hugh, but it sustained him. He learnt again to suspend his hopes and fears, and to leave all confidently in the hands of God; and time, too, had its healing balm; the bitter loss, by soft gradations, became a sweet and loving memory, and a memory that sweetened the thought of the dark world whither too he must sometime turn his steps. For if indeed our individuality endures, he could realise that one who loved so purely, so loyally, so intensely, would not fail him on the other side of the silent river, but would welcome him with unabated love, perhaps only feeling a tender wonder that those who yet had the passage to make should find it to be so terrible, so unendurable.

VII

Liberty — Cambridge — Literary Work — Egotism

The question which, when he resigned his appointment, occupied Hugh, was where he should live. He would have preferred to settle in the country, loving, as he did, silence and pure air, woods and fields. He had never liked London, though it had become endurable to him by familiarity. He decided, however, that at first, at all events, he must if possible find a place where he could see a certain amount of society, and where he would be able to obtain the books he expected to need. He was afraid that if he transferred himself at once to the country, he might sink into a morbid seclusion, as he had no strong sociable impulses. His thoughts naturally turned to his own university. He thought that if he could find a small house at Cambridge, suitable to his means, he would be able to have as much or as little society as he desired, while at the same time he would be on the edge of the country. Moreover the flat fenland, which is generally supposed to be unattractive, had always possessed a peculiar charm for Hugh. He spent some time at home, revelling in his freedom, while he made inquiries for a house. The thought of a long perspective of days before him, without fixed engagements, without responsibilities, so that he could come and go as he pleased, filled him with delight.

His father had not at all disapproved of the decision. Hugh had shown him that he was pecuniarily independent; but he was aware that in the background of his father's mind lay the hope that, even so late in life, he might still be drawn to enter the ministry of the Church. At all events he thought that Hugh might gain some academical position; and thus he gave a decidedly cordial assent to the change, only expressing a hope that Hugh would not make a hurried decision.

Hugh did not delay to sketch out a plan of work. But whereas before he had worked only when he could, he now found himself in the blessed position of being able to work when he would. Instead of becoming, as he had feared, desultory, he found that his work exercised a strong attraction over him—indeed that it became for him, with an amazing swiftness, the one pursuit in the world about which exercise, food, amusement, grouped themselves as secondary accessories. This was no doubt in part accounted for by the fact that he had acquired a habit of regular work, a craving for steady occupation; but it was also far more due to the fact that Hugh had really, and almost as though by accident, discovered his ruling passion. He was in truth a writer, a word-artist; his only fear was, whether, in the hard-worked unmitigated years of specified toil, he had not perhaps lost the requisite mental agility, whether he had not failed to acquire the elastic use of words, the almost instinctive sense of colour and motion in language, which can only be won through constant and even unsuccessful use. That remained to be seen; and meanwhile his plans settled themselves. He found a small, picturesque, irregularly-built house crushed in between the road and the river, which in fact dipped its very feet in the stream; from its quaint oriel and gallery, Hugh could look down, on a bright day, into the clear heart of the water, and survey its swaying reeds and poising fish. The house was near the centre of the town; yet from its back windows it overlooked a long green stretch of rough pastureland, now a common, and once a fen, which came like a long green finger straight into the very heart of the town. There was a great sluice a few yards away, through which the river poured into a wide reach of stream, so that the air was always musical with the sound of falling water, the murmur of which could be heard on still nights through the shuttered and curtained casements. The sun, on the short winter days, used to set, in smouldering glory, behind the long lines of leafless trees which terminated the fen; and in summer the little wooded peninsula that formed part of a neighbouring garden, was rich in leaf, and loud with the song of birds. The little house had, in fact, the poetical quality, and charmed the eye and ear at every turn, the whisper of the little weir outside seeming to brim with sweet contented sound every corner of the quaint, irregular, and low-ceiled rooms, with their large beams and dark corners.

So Hugh settled here after his emancipation, and for the first time in his life realised what it meant to be free. He woke day after day to the sensation that he had no engagements, no ties; that he could arrange his hours of work and liberty as he liked, go where he would; that no one would question his right, interfere with his independence, or even take the least interest in his movements. His freedom was at first, to his dismay, something of a burden to him; he had been used to ceaseless interruptions, multifarious engagements; the one struggle, the one preoccupation, had been to win a few hours for solitude, for reflection, for literary work. But now that the whole of time was at his disposal, he found himself unable to concentrate his mind, to apply himself. He had several friends at Cambridge; but the strain of making new acquaintances, of familiarising himself with the temperaments and the tastes of the new set of personalities, was very great. It was impossible for Hugh to enter upon neutral, civil, colourless relations. He could not meet a man or a woman without endeavouring to find some common ground of sympathy and understanding. And this was made more difficult to him at Cambridge by the swift monotony in which the years had flowed away. Time seemed to have stood still there in those twenty years. Many of the men that he remembered seemed still to be there, contentedly pursuing the customary round, circulating from their rooms to Hall, from Hall to Combination-room, and back again. Thus Hugh, picking up the thread where he had laid it down, appeared to himself to be youthful, inexperienced, insignificant; while to those who made his acquaintance he seemed to be a grave and serious man of affairs, with a standing in the world and a definite line of his own.

Thus the first months were months of some depression. Not that he would have gone back if he could, or that he ever doubted of the wisdom, the inevitableness of the step; even in moments of dejection it cheered him to feel that he was not eating his heart out in fruitless work, or solemnly performing a duty, which relied for seriousness upon its outer place in a settled scheme, rather than upon any intrinsic value that it possessed. But his life soon settled down into a steady routine. He gave his morning to letters, business, and reading; his afternoons to exercise, his evenings to writing and academical sociabilities. His aim began gradually to be to make the most of the sacred hours of the late afternoon, when his mind was most alert, and when he seemed to possess the easiest mastery of language. He consecrated those hours to his chosen work, and it was his object to fit himself, as by a species of training, to make the most and best of that good time, which lay like gold among the débris of the day. It seemed to him that the solid, unimaginative work of the morning cleared away a certain heaviness and sluggishness of apprehension, which was the shadow of sleep; that the open air, the active movement of the afternoon, removed the clumsier and grosser insistence of the body; and that there resulted a frame of mind, when the imagination was lively and alert, and when the willing brain served out its stores with a cordial rapidity. There was a danger perhaps of selfish absorption in such a scheme of life; but at least no artist ever more sedulously cultivated the best and most fruitful conditions for the practice of his art. Hugh grew to have an almost morbid sense of the value of time. Interruptions, social entertainments, engagements which interfered with his programme, he resented and resolutely avoided. He became indeed aware that other people, to whom the value of his work was not apparent, were apt to regard the jealous arrangement of his hours as the mere whim of a self-absorbed dilettante. But that troubled Hugh little, because he realised that his only hope of doing sound and worthy work lay in making a sacrifice of the ordinary and trifling occupations of life, of forming definite habits, for the want of which so many capable and brilliant persons sink into unproductiveness.

Yet the life had a danger which Hugh did not at first perceive. It tended to concentrate his thoughts too much upon himself. His writings took on a personal colour, a warm, self-regarding light, of which his candid friends did not hesitate to make him aware. The bitterness of the slow progress of a book, and of the long time that must elapse between its execution and its appearance, is that the readers of it tend to consider that it reflects the exact contemporary thought of its writer. Hugh's mind and personality grew fast in those days; and by the time that his friends were criticising a book as the outcome of his immediate thought, he was feeling himself that it was but a milestone on the road, marking a spot that he had left leagues behind him.

But the creative instinct, which had struggled fitfully with the hard practical conditions of his professional life, now took a sudden bound forward. His writing became the one important thing in the world for Hugh. He had gained, he found, through constant practice, dry as the labour had been, a considerable fluency and firmness of touch: now sentences shaped themselves under his hand like living things; words flowed easily from their abundant reservoir. Yet the peril, which he soon grew to perceive, was that his outfit of emotional experience, his knowledge of human life in its breadth and complexity, was very narrow and limited. He had seen life only under a single aspect, and that an aspect which, poignant and intense as it was, did not easily lend itself to artistic treatment. The result was that his outlook was a narrow one, and his mind was driven back upon itself. The need to speak, to express, to shape thoughts in appropriate words, so long repressed, so instinctive to him, became almost fearfully imperative. He was haunted by a hundred ardent speculations in art, in literature, in religion, in metaphysics, all of a vague rather than a precise kind. His mind had been always of a loose, poetical type, turning to the quality of things rather than to outward facts or practical questions. Temperaments, individualities, appealed to him more than national movements or aspirations; and then the old love of nature came back like a solemn passion.

This sudden growth of egotism and introspection tended to alarm and disquiet Hugh's friends; they put it down to his severance from practical activities, and began to fear a morbid and self-regarding attitude. Yet Hugh knew that it would right itself; it was but the completion of a process, begun in his college days, and checked by his early entry into professional life; it was a return of his youth, the natural fulfilment of that period of speculative thought, which a young man must pass through before he can put himself in line with the world. And in any case it was inevitable; and Hugh was content as before to leave himself in the hand of God, only glad at least that a process which would naturally have been finished under the overshadowing of the melancholy of youth, could thus be worked out with the temperate tranquillity, the serenity of manhood.

VIII

Foundations of Faith—Duality—Christianity—
The Will of God

After all the inevitable bustle, the moving and settling of furniture, the constant noting of small needs, the conferences with tradesmen, all the details inseparable from establishing a new home, had died away, Hugh found himself, as has been said, for the first time in his life in comparative solitude. He had a few old friends in Cambridge; but unless two men are members of the same college, meetings, in a place of many small engagements, have to be deliberately arranged. Hugh could always go and dine in the hall of his college, and be certain of finding there a quiet good-fellowship and a pleasant tolerance. But he had not as yet mastered the current of little incidents which furnish so much of the conversation of small societies: allusions to facts familiar to all beside himself were perpetually being made; and he knew that nothing is so tiresome as a would-be sympathetic questioner, who does not understand the precise lie of the ground. He had as yet no definite work; a literary task in which he was shortly to be engaged had not as yet begun; the materials had not been placed in his hands. Thus compelled by circumstances to pass through a period of enforced retreat, Hugh resolved upon a certain course of action. He determined to put down in writing, for his own instruction and benefit, the precise position he held in thought—his hopes, his desires, his beliefs. He set to work, it must be confessed, in a melancholy mood, the melancholy that is inseparable from the position of a man who has lived a very full and active life, and from whom the burden of activities is suddenly lifted. Though the lifting of the weight was an immense relief, and though he could often summon back cheerfulness by reflecting how entire his freedom was, and how troublesomely he would have been occupied if he had still held his professional position, yet the mere fact that there was no longer any necessity to brace his energies and faculties to meet some particular call of duty, gave him spaces of a flaccid dreariness, in which his accustomed literary work palled on him; one could not read or write for ever; and so he set himself, as I have said, to compose a memorandum, a *symbol*, so to speak, of his moral and intellectual faith.

He was surprised, as soon as he began his task, to find how much of what he had believed to be certainties shrank and dwindled. A perfect sincerity with himself was the only possible condition under which such a work was worth undertaking. A sincerity which should resolutely discard all that was merely traditional and customary, should emphasise nothing, should regard nothing as proved, in which hope outran scientific certainty.

He found then that his creed began with a deep and abiding faith in God; he believed, that is, in the existence of an all-pervading, all-powerful Will, lying behind and in the scheme of things.

Side by side with this belief, and inextricably interwoven with it, was his belief in his own identity and personality. That was perhaps the only thing of which he was ultimately assured. But his experience of the world was that it was peopled by similar personalities, each of whom seemed equally conscious of a separate existence, who were swayed by motives similar in kind, though differing in detail, from the motives which swayed himself; beyond these personalities, lay whole ranges of sentient beings, which sank at last, by slow and minute gradations, into matter which seemed to him to be inanimate; but even all this was permeated by certain forces, themselves unseen, but the symptoms of which were apparent in all directions, such as heat, motion, attraction, electricity. He believed it possible that all these might be different manifestations and specimens of the same central force; but it was nothing more than a vague possibility.

He was next confronted with a mysterious fact. In every day and hour of his own life he was brought face to face with a double experience. At moments he felt himself full of life, health, and joy; at other moments he felt himself equally subject to torpor, *malaise*, and suffering. What it was that made these two classes of experience clear to him he could not tell; but there was no questioning the fact that at times he was the subject of experience of a pleasant kind, which he would have prolonged if he could; while at times he was equally conscious of experiences which his only desire was to terminate as speedily as possible.

This mystery, which no philosopher had ever explained, seemed to him to run equally through the whole of nature. He asked himself whether he was in the presence of two warring forces. Would the Will, whatever it was, which produced happiness, have made that happiness permanent, if it could? was it thwarted by some other power, perhaps equally strong—though it seemed to Hugh that the happiness of most sentient beings decidedly and largely predominated over their unhappiness—a power which was deliberately inimical to joy and peace, health and well-being?

It seemed to him, however, that the two were so inextricably intermingled, and so closely ministered, the one to the other, that there was an essential unity of Will at work; and that both joyful and painful experiences were the work of the same mind. He therefore rejected at the outset the belief that what was commonly called evil could be a principle foreign to the nature of the Will of God; and he put aside as childish the belief that evil is created by the faculty of human choice, setting itself against the benevolent Will of God; for benevolence thus hampered would at once become a mere tame and ineffective desire for the welfare of sentient things, and be wholly deprived of all the attributes of omnipotence. Besides, he saw the same qualities that produced suffering in humanity, such as the instincts of cruelty, lust, self-preservation, manifesting themselves with equal force among those sentient creatures which did not seem to be capable of exercising any moral choice.

But in regarding nature, as revealed by the researches of scientists, he saw that there was a slow development taking place, a development of infinite patience and almost insupportable delay. Finer and finer became the organisation of animal life; and in the development of human life, too, he saw a slow progress, a daily deepening power of organising natural resources to gratify increasingly complicated needs. Not only was an energy at work, but a progressive energy, bringing into existence things that were not, and revealing secrets unknown before.

He next attempted to define his moral belief; and here, too, he saw in the world a progressive force at work. He saw society becoming more and more refined, more desirous to amend faulty conditions, more anxious to alleviate pain; and this not only with self-regarding motives, but with a vital sympathy, which reached its height in the deliberate purpose of many individuals that, even if condemned to suffer themselves, they would yet spend thought and energy in relieving, if possible, the ills of others.

He saw in the teaching of Christ what appeared to be the purest and simplest attempt ever made to formulate unselfish affection. No teacher of morals had ever reached the point of inculcating upon men the belief that it was the highest joy to spend the energies of life in contributing to the happiness of others. Though he saw in the system of Christ, as popularised and interpreted, a whole host of insecure assumptions, unverified assertions, and even degrading traditions, yet he could not doubt of the Divine force of the central message. If he was not in a position to affirm with certitude the truth of the recorded events which attended the origin of the Christian revelation, he could yet affirm with confidence that in the teaching of Christ a higher range of emotion had been reached than had ever been approached before; and he saw that spirit, in countless regions, however slowly, leavening the thought, the instincts of the world. The question then resolved itself into a practical one. How in his own life was he to make the serenity, the happiness which he desired, predominate over the suffering, the discontent to which he was liable? Could it be done by an effort of mind? His professional life had shown him that activity had not brought him any peace of mind, principally because the system which he was bound to serve demanded such immense expense of labour for purely unprofitable ends. It had not been part of the humble and necessary work of the world, which must be done by some one, if human beings are to live at all; it had only been the outcome of the needlessly elaborate life of a highly organised community. It had filled his life full of a futile intellectual toil. And then, the effect upon his own character had been to hamper and stunt his natural energies. It had given him false ideals and wrong motives.

Looking back at his own life, Hugh saw that ambition, in one form or another, had poisoned his spirit. He saw that the instinct to gain a supremacy at the expense of others had been the one serious motive pressed upon him from first to last; indeed the necessity for moral control had been really, though not nominally, urged upon him, on the ground that by yielding to bodily desires he would be likely to frustrate his visions of success. Only of late had he had any suspicion of the truth, that gentleness, peacefulness, kindness, sincerity, quiet toil, activity of body and mind, were the things that really made life sweet and joyful. Had he learned it too late to be able to exorcise the demons that had so long harboured in his soul? He feared so.

But at last, after long pondering, he arrived at his decision, which was that if indeed this vast and patient Will was in the background of all, the only way was to follow it, to lean upon it; above all things not to be distracted by the conventions of society, which, though they too, in a sense, had their origin in the Will of God, yet were things to be left behind, to be struggled out of. There might indeed be some natures to which such things were attractive and satisfying, but Hugh had no doubt that though they might attract him, they could not satisfy.

And yet over his thoughts there brooded the shadow of the sad possibilities that lay in wait for him, and of which he had already felt the touch — pain, weariness, a discontented mind, jealousy, despair, and at the end of all death, which closed the prospect whichever way he looked. But if these things too were of the very nature of God, His Will indeed, though obscure and terrible, the only way was in a patient and loving submission, a knowledge that they could not be wholly in vain; and so he resolved that his life should be even so; that he would embrace all opportunities of showing kindness, giving help to others; that he would live a simple life of labour, using his faculties to the uttermost, as God should provide; and that his whole being should be a deliberate prayer that he might do the Will of God as affected himself, without seeking the praise or recognition of men. He foresaw indeed much solitude, much weariness. God had never given him one whom he could unreservedly love, though He had sent him abundance of pure and noble friendships. Quiet dependence upon God, simplicity of life, a readiness to serve, a strenuous use of the gifts given to him; that was the faith in which Hugh, now late in life, and after what profitless squandering of energies, began his pilgrimage.

Art — The End of Art

It seemed strange to Hugh to sit there as he did, in his quiet house beside the stream, with an active professional life behind him, and wonder what the next act would be. His time was now filled with an editorial task which would demand all his energies, or rather a large part of them; but editorial work, however interesting in itself — and the interest of his particular work was great — left one part of the mind unsatisfied; that part of the mind which desired to create some beautiful thing. Hugh's difficulty was this, that he had no very urgent message, to use a dignified word, to deliver to the world. Nowadays, to appeal to the world, it is necessary to do things, it would seem, in rather a strident way, to blow a trumpet, or wave a flag, or command an army, or reform a department of state, or control a railroad. Hugh had neither the power nor the will to write a virile book or a powerful story, or to take imagination captive. He did not wish to head a revolt against anything in particular. The day of the old, grim, sinister tyrannies, he felt, in the western corner of the world, was over, and the kind of tyranny that vexed his spirit was a far more secret and subtle distortion of liberty. It was the rule of conventionality that he desired to destroy, the appetite for luxury, and power, and excitement, and strong sensation. He would have liked to do something to win men back to the joys that were within the reach of all, the joys of peaceful work, and simplicity, and friendship, and quiet hopefulness. These were what seemed to Hugh to be the staple of life, and to be within the reach of so many people. And yet he had no mission. He could only detest the loud voices of the world and its feverish excitements, with all his heart; and on the other hand he loved with increasing contentment the gentler and beautiful background of life, that enacted itself every day in garden and field and wood; the quiet waiting things, the old church seen over orchards and cottage-roofs, the deep pool in the reedy river, dreaming its own quiet dreams, whatever passed in the noisy world. He was sure that those things would bring peace to many weary spirits, if they could but learn to love them.

Artists and musicians, Hugh felt, were the happiest of all people; for they made the beautiful thing that might stand by itself, without need of comment. The graceful boy or girl that they painted, undimmed by age and evil experience, looked down at you from the canvas with a pure and radiant smile, and became as it were a spring of clear water, where a soul might bathe and be clean. Or the picture of some silent woodland place, some lilied pool on a golden summer afternoon—how the peace of it came into the spirit, how it seemed to assure the heart that God loved beauty best, lavishing it with an unwearied hand, even where there could be none to behold it but Himself! Then the musician,—how he wove the airy stuff of sound, so that the pathos of the world, its heavy mysteries, its sunlit joys, started into life, embracing the soul, and bidding it not be faithless or blind. These were the pure gifts of art, the spells before which the dull conventions of the world, its noise and dust, crumbled into the ugly ashes that they really were.

Beside those magical secrets the clumsy art of the writer stood abashed. Those tints, those notes were such definite things; but in the grosser and more tainted medium with which writers dealt, where so much depended upon association and point of view, there was so much less certainty of producing the effect intended, that one faltered and lost faith. One thing was certain, that it was useless to *search* for a mission; the purpose must descend from heaven, as the eagle pounced on Ganymede, and carry the trembling and awed minister high above the heads of men. But the only thing that the faithful writer could do was to map out some little piece of quiet work, make no vast design, seek for no large sovereignty; and then work patiently on with ever-present enjoyment, learning his art, gaining skill and mastery over his vast and complex instrument, till he gained certainty of touch and the power of saying, with perfect lucidity, with pure transparency of phrase, exactly what he meant; and then, behind his art, to live resolutely in his simple creed, whatever article of it he could master, sure of this, that if his inspiration

came, he would be able to present it worthily; and if it did not
come — well, his would have been a grave, quiet, gracious life, lik